For Rufus—T.M.

KINGFISHER
LONDON & NEW YORK

Text copyright © Tony Mitton 2021
Illustrations copyright © Ant Parker 2021
Designed by Anthony Hannant (LittleRedAnt) 2021

Published in the United States by Kingfisher,
120 Broadway, New York, NY 10271
Kingfisher is an imprint of Macmillan Children's Books, London.
All rights reserved
Distributed in the U.S. and Canada by Macmillan, 120 Broadway, New York, NY 10271

LIBRARY OF CONGRESS CATALOGING-IN-PUBLICATION DATA HAS BEEN APPLIED FOR

ISBN 978-0-7534-7654-3 (Hardback)

Kingfisher books are available for special promotions and premiums. For details contact:
Special Markets Department, Macmillan, 120 Broadway, New York, NY 10271

For more information, please visit
www.kingfisherbooks.com

Printed in China
9 8 7 6 5 4 3 2 1

BIG BULLDOZERS

Tony Mitton
and Ant Parker

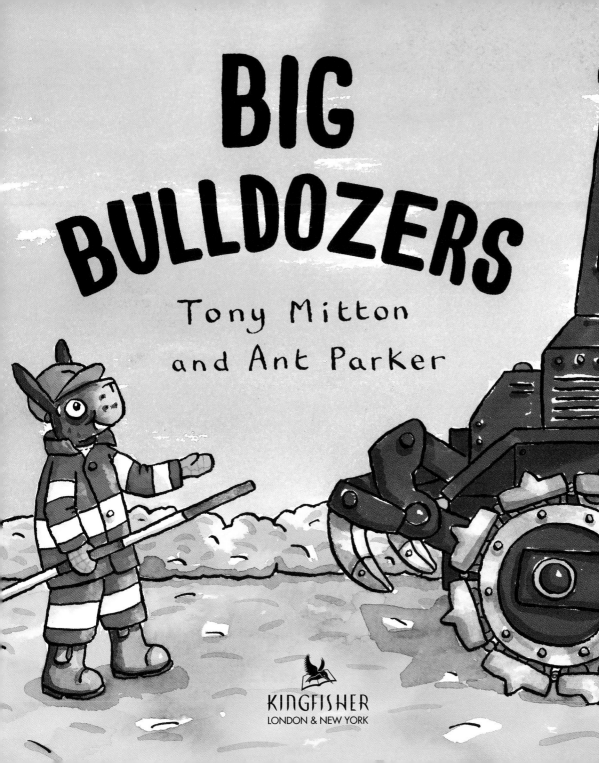

KINGFISHER
LONDON & NEW YORK

crawler tracks

Here's a busy bulldozer.
See how it's made:
Tough crawler tracks
and a strong metal blade.

blade

The crawler tracks travel
over all kinds of ground
while the powerful blade
pushes rubble around.

The blade has a cutting edge
for breaking up lumps.
The tracks have treads
for riding over bumps.

The blade tilts down
for digging up earth
or lifts up to push things
for all that it's worth.

ripper

A bulldozer often has
a ripper at the rear.
The ripper breaks ground up
that's too hard to clear.

The ripper has a shank
that cuts through the rough,
and then the blade can shunt it
easily enough.

The cab has a seat
where the operator sits.
From there they can work
all the different bits.

The operator drives
their dozer along.
A bulldozer engine
has to be strong.

A bulldozer's job
is to level and clear.

See how it's smoothing
the ground out here.

And look here's another
on a very lumpy site

spreading out the garbage
till it's laid out right.

If there's been a storm
and it's blown down trees,
a bulldozer clears up
the damage with ease.

A tree-clearing bulldozer
has all the force
to shift fallen trees
and earth, of course.

If you've a road
that's blocked with snow,
a bulldozer's blade
can shift it . . . so!

Or an ordinary truck
can be used to snow-shunt
if you get a blade
that fits on the front.

If there's a job
in a very tight place,

a baby bulldozer
might fit the space!

But though some bulldozers
may be small . . .

this big bulldozer towers up tall!

Bulldozer bits

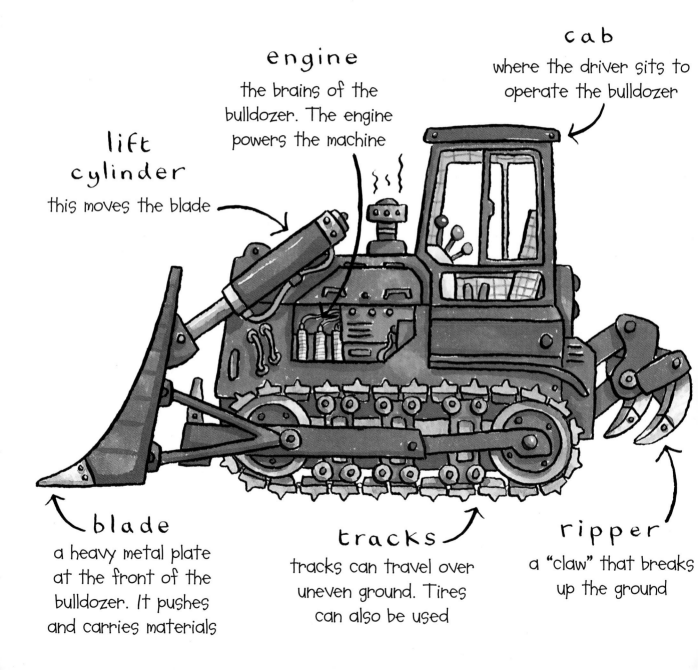

engine
the brains of the bulldozer. The engine powers the machine

cab
where the driver sits to operate the bulldozer

lift cylinder
this moves the blade

blade
a heavy metal plate at the front of the bulldozer. It pushes and carries materials

tracks
tracks can travel over uneven ground. Tires can also be used

ripper
a "claw" that breaks up the ground

Look out for these **AMAZING** books by Tony Mitton and Ant Parker!

Collect all the **AMAZING MACHINES** picture story books:

Or store them all in the **BIG TRUCKLOAD OF FUN**— the perfect gift for little ones:

Contains 14 Amazing Machines picture story books

Meet your favorite animals with the **AMAZING ANIMALS** series: